P9-DUY-547

PENGUINS

PENGUINS

Wolfgang Kaehler

Chronicle Books • San Francisco

Library of Congress Cataloging in Publication Data
Kaehler, Wolfgang.
    Penguins / by Wolfgang Kaehler.
        p.   cm.
    ISBN 0-87701-649-6.
    ISBN 0-87701-637-2 (pbk.)
    1. Penguins. I. Title.
QL696.S5K34   1989
598.4′41—dc20   89-31316
                        CIP

Book and cover design: Nancy Webb

Distributed in Canada by
Raincoast Books
112 East Third Avenue
Vancouver, B.C.
V5T 1C8

10   9   8   7   6   5   4   3   2

Chronicle Books
275 Fifth Street
San Francisco, California
94103

Printed in Japan

Previous page: Lemaire Channel, Antarctic Peninsula.

ACKNOWLEDGMENTS

I would like to give special thanks to Danita Delimont, who has worked with me and my photography for many years, and to the millions of penguins who made this book possible.

Chinstrap penguins resting on blue iceberg.

PERSONAL ENCOUNTERS WITH PENGUINS

It was a warm spring day in the Falklands. I was walking over a mossy plain on New Island, surrounded by hills covered with tussock grass. Ahead of me, a steep cliff fell four hundred feet straight down toward a windblown ocean. A heavy surf was crashing against jagged, polished rocks, the noise amplified by the walls of a canyon.

But another sound challenged that of the ocean. I could hear raucous calls, sometimes building up to a high pitched squeaking. As I approached the cliff, the sound grew louder and louder. Coming up a little hill I could suddenly see a huge area where no vegetation was growing. The evening sunshine made it appear almost yellow. Countless black dots stood out against this bare spot; some were moving. This was the special moment I had dreamed of as a child: I had reached my first penguin colony. My fascination for penguins had begun years back while watching a movie on Antarctica. Now, as I stood before these comical creatures in their natural habitat, I knew this was a day that I would never forget.

I sat on a rock surrounded by more than twenty thousand rockhopper penguins. A few black-browed albatrosses were nesting among the penguins, and to the right of the colony, a group of king cormorants had established their breeding territories. Some of the rockhopper penguins were incubating their eggs. Others were still busy building rather disorderly nests using dried bits of tussock grass, small stones, and feathers. The penguins guarded their nests to prevent neighbors from stealing a pebble or other building materials. If a thief was caught in the act, a loud screaming broke out. Unfortunately I could not understand their language, and I had no reply when a penguin jumped onto my foot and tried to pull out the laces of my shoes, to use for its nest. Since this encounter in 1977 I have returned to Antarctica and the Sub-Antarctic islands more than a dozen times to observe and photograph many varieties of delightful penguins.

I have always found the way penguins walk rather amusing. With their short feet, they are quite clumsy: some waddle, others hop, and, in order to cross a field of snow or ice, many will toboggan on their bellies. These flightless birds are better adapted to a life at sea than on land. In the water a penguin is in its element. Its wings are used as flippers, and it "flies" underwater at the very rapid speed of ten knots or more. Penguins come ashore only to breed and to molt.

There are seventeen species of penguins, all of them in the southern hemisphere. I am often asked if I have a favorite species. It is hard to say. The appearance, behavior, and mentality of each species is unique. One species I have enjoyed a great deal is the chinstrap. As their name indicates, they have a marking that resembles a strap over their chin, making them look as though they are constantly smiling. Once, as I walked alongside a chinstrap colony, some of the penguins began crossing right in front of me, almost running over my feet. One of the chinstraps stopped and looked up at me. It stretched itself as tall as possible and then began to croak at me in its not very musical voice. I think I understood the message: "What are you doing in my path? Can't you see that I have the right of way?" I stepped back and the penguin appeared to be pleased and continued on its way, still growling as it went.

On another occasion, I was walking along the beach on Paulet Island, off the Antarctic Peninsula. Slightly uphill, about five yards from me, was the edge of an Adélie penguin colony. Most of the penguins were incubating their eggs. Suddenly one Adélie came racing down the gravel hill toward me. It ran right up to me, pressed its breast against my leg, hammered my knee with its beak, and began beating my leg with its flippers. I was amazed at how powerful its flippers and beak were. I could feel them sharply through three layers of warm clothing. Shaking my leg I tried to rid myself of this attacker. I thought about the numerous territorial fights I had watched between nesting penguins: if their biting and slapping hurt me, how much more would it hurt another penguin, which is much smaller than I am?

While the timing and duration of the cycle varies with each species, an Adélie penguin colony comes to life at the beginning of the austral summer, around October, when its breeding season starts. After the sea ice begins to break up, the male penguins are the first to arrive at the nest site to establish their territories and prepare their nests for the females. Once a site is established it needs to be defended against neighboring or late arriving penguins. Nests in the middle of the colony are preferable because they provide greater protection from some predators, such as skuas. When the first females arrive, the activity and noise level in the colony increases substantially. Loud greetings are heard everywhere, and courtship activities begin. About twenty-five days later, usually in early November, each couple lays its first egg, followed by a second egg about three days later. Both parents share incubating and feeding responsibilities. Usually the male incubates the eggs first, while the female goes off to feed at sea. With one of the parents gone from each nest, the colony is tranquil, the incubating penguins usually sitting quietly on their eggs. Now the skuas—brown, gull-like birds that are predatory to penguin colonies—try to trick the penguins into leaving their nests so they can snatch the eggs or small chicks. Skuas even pair up to be more successful.

After the female has spent a few days feeding at sea, it returns to the nest to relieve its partner from incubation duty. The arriving partner may also bring a gift of a small stone, which gets piled onto the nest. Each time, before a partner takes over incubation, a nest relief ceremony takes place. The two penguins stretch their necks, point their beaks straight into the air, wave their heads back and forth, and let out boisterous cries. Then they simultaneously point their beaks toward the ground, displaying the black crest above their necks. With their eyes wide open they let out a growling sound. Slowly they raise their heads as the sound continues to grow louder. When their wide open beaks are pointing straight into the air, there is a break in the ritual. Both penguins are quiet for a moment before starting the same ritual all over again. Finally the bird that returned from the sea steps behind the partner and moves onto the nest, placing the eggs under its brood patch. The other penguin, relieved from duty, goes off to sea. This ceremony, scientists believe, reinforces recognition between partners.

By the beginning of December a fine peeping sound can be heard in the Adélie colonies. After about thirty-three days of incubation a chick begins to hatch. First it pecks a small hole through the egg shell, then enlarges it bit by bit until it is able to crawl out. Immediately it is sheltered by its parent for protection from predators and the cold. Keeping the newly hatched chicks warm is very important, especially if a cold wind blows or a blizzard covers the colony with snow. At any time during the brief austral summer, the temperatures can suddenly drop below freezing. Covered by the warm feathers of a parent the new generation is barely visible to an observer. As time passes the peeping gets louder and louder, and little beaks poke out from under parents' bellies. The chicks are hungry and ready to be fed. A chick will stretch its head up in the air and then tap its beak against the beak of the parent. This is a signal for mom or dad to open up their beak.

Once the parent has obliged, the chick's little head almost disappears inside. Penguin chicks are always hungry: they feed often and grow rapidly.

After the chicks reach the age of about three weeks, they form small groups called creches or kindergartens. In these groups the chicks gain protection from skua attacks. They also huddle close together for warmth. For the first time both parents are able to leave the nest site to feed at sea. The adults line up along the shore in groups, cautiously watching for leopard seals and killer whales. These predators often swim along the beach in front of penguin colonies, waiting for penguins. More and more penguins line up and the group becomes restless. The birds in front stretch their necks to get a better view of the water, while those in the back push forward. Suddenly the first dives into the water. The others quickly follow, creating a waterfall of penguins. While swimming they stay in protective groups. Most penguins feed on krill, squid, and small fish. After they return to land from feeding, the adults look for a quiet spot on the shore, where they rest before going back to the colony to feed their chicks.

Parents and chicks recognize each other by their voices. Once the chick identifies its parent, it leaves the creche and runs toward the adult to beg for food. Sometimes the chick is too pushy and the adult runs away, pursued by the persistent chick. This food chase often goes through the entire colony. Finally the adult stops and regurgitates food to feed its chick.

After about twenty-five days the chicks begin to molt. They lose their furry down slowly until they are about forty days old, when only a few wisps of down remain around the head. In their new juvenile dress, they will soon leave the colony and go to sea. Having completed the task of raising the young, the adults will return to sea to store up with food for themselves. The adults will return to shore for the last time in the summer in order to molt. Finally, with new feathers, they go back to sea, where they will spend the winter.

Each species of penguin has a different breeding cycle, behavior pattern, and nesting habitat. Some species nest in burrows, while others nest above ground. The colonies vary in size, from just a few nests to more than a million. About twenty-five thousand king penguins nest in one large colony on South Georgia Island. A king penguin colony of this size is an amazing and exciting sight. I have sat all day in one spot studying these colorful birds. King penguin chicks are particularly curious. Often they walked right up to me and pecked at my parka, or wandered over to check out my equipment bag. It was great fun to watch as they discovered their reflection in the skylight filter of my lens: they stretched out their necks and tapped with their beaks against the filter.

I am always amazed by the mile-long chinstrap colony on Deception Island. One part of this volcanic island is covered with penguins as far as the eye can see. The colony stretches way up, almost to the highest point of the island. It is hard to imagine how long it takes for a chinstrap to walk up to the highest nest of the colony: it took me about forty-five minutes, and my legs are quite a bit longer!

Antarctica and the Sub-Antarctic regions are the home not only for penguins but also for many other species of wildlife. A variety of seabirds build their nests here during the summer; huge numbers of seals inhabit the beaches and pack ice; and in bays and fjord-like channels, whales spout and breech. The Antarctic Ocean needs to be very rich in food to support the abundance of seabirds and mammals.

Up until recently this continent has remained the last truly pristine place in the world. Man has been able to protect it from exploitation, but its future is uncertain. More and more attention is being drawn to this continent, where enormous deposits of natural resources are believed to exist. One oil spill could kill millions of penguins and other life forms. The mining of minerals not only would ruin this unspoiled landscape, it could also destroy the breeding grounds of the wildlife. Let us be vigilant and hope that this never happens, so that many years from now a rockhopper penguin will be able to jump on our grandchildren's feet and pull out the shoelaces for nesting material.

Wolfgang Kaehler
February 7, 1989

Above: A chinstrap penguin colony. Penguin colonies vary in size from a few pairs to more than a million.

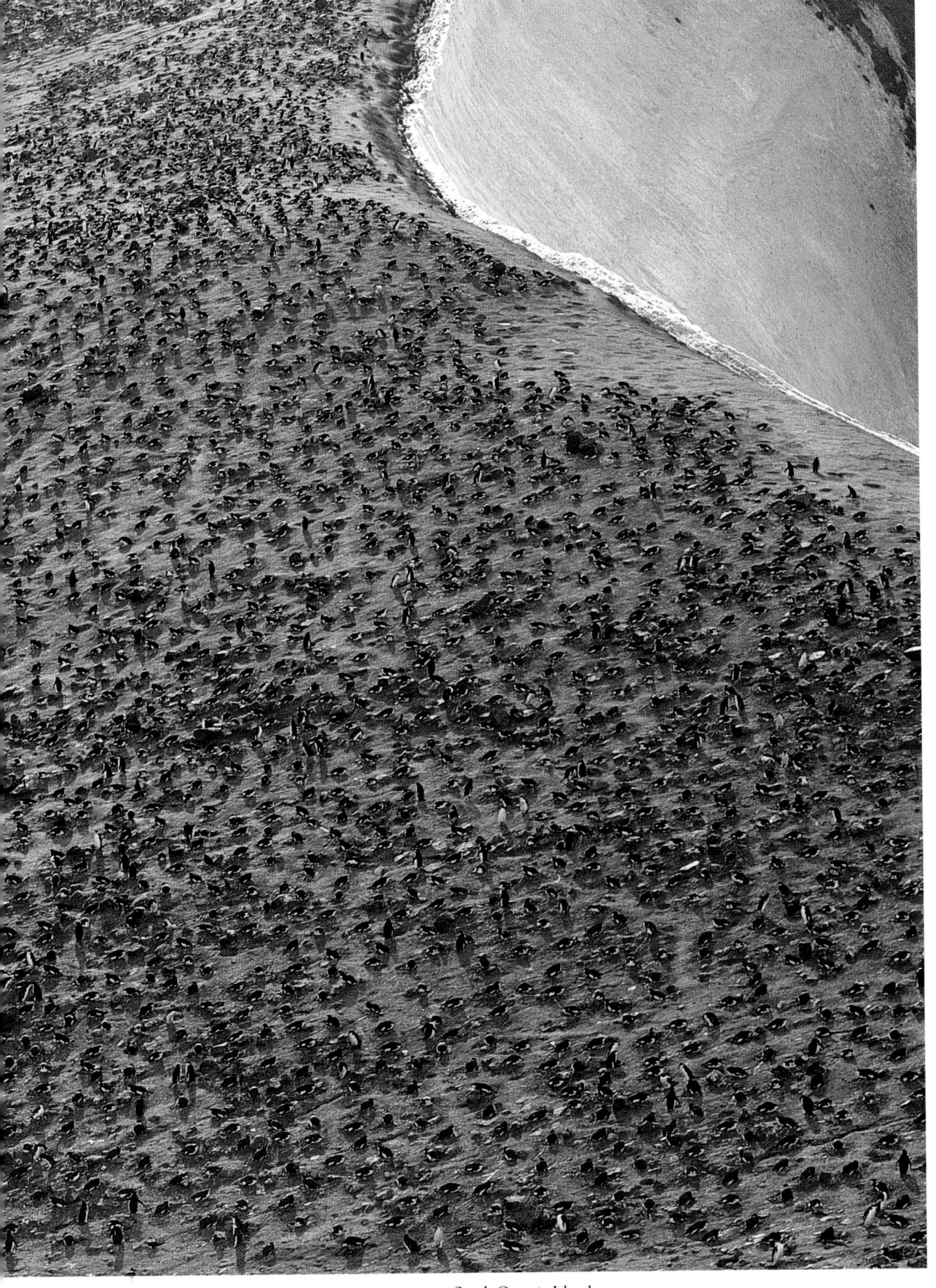

Next pages: About 25,000 king penguin pairs nesting on South Georgia Island.

Left: These nesting king penguins are incubating single eggs, balanced on the upper surfaces of their feet. The incubation period for king penguins is about fifty-four days.

Above: King penguins are easily distinguished by their bright yellow-orange markings on the upper chest, head, and lower beak. They can grow to three feet in height.

Above: Royal penguins, with slicked-back yellow crest feathers, only nest on Macquarie Island, south of Australia.

Right: Rockhoppers are the smallest of the crested penguins, averaging about five pounds, though weight varies with the season.

Rockhopper penguins have bright red eyes and often appear comical due to their spiky head feathers.

Above: Macaroni penguins also belong to the family of crested penguins. They nest here, on the Falkland Islands, and throughout the Antarctic.

Right: These rockhoppers found an unusual spot for preening each other—an abandoned black-browed albatross nest.

Chinstrap penguins. These all-black-and-white penguins were named for the unique markings on their chin.

Left: An Adélie penguin.

Above: Adélie penguins on ice and snow covered beach, Antarctica. They are watching for dangerous predators before diving into the sea.

Previous pages: An Adélie penguin shakes its head and excretes a concentrated salt solution after drinking sea water. Penguins are seabirds and have a gland that processes out the salt in the water.

Above and right: Adélie penguins. Penguins are birds with feathered flippers instead of wings. They use their flippers to propel themselves through the water and to get rid of excess heat. A dense layer of waterproof feathers plays a vital role in keeping them warm.

Above: As spring arrives, Antarctic pack ice begins to break up, and penguins return to their nesting colonies.

Next pages: A penguin, uncharacteristically alone, is struggling over the pack ice in search of open water and a chance to return to its companions.

Previous pages: Due to melting and eroding, this tabular iceberg turned upside down, and penguins were able to climb up its gentle slope. Mt. Bransfield, on the Antarctic Peninsula, is in the background.

Above: During winter (March to October), penguins return to the sea, from time to time resting on icebergs or ice floes. Here Adélie and chinstrap penguins share a small iceberg.

Left: Chinstrap penguins resting along the shore.

Above: A group of Adélie penguins porpoising in and out of the water to breathe while feeding on krill at sea. In water, penguins are in their element; they are swift swimmers and skillful divers.

29

Previous pages and above: Returning from feeding at sea is often quite difficult. These rockhopper penguins in the Falkland Islands have to fight heavy surf to reach the shore. Before returning to the nest site, they will dry and preen their feathers.

Right: Rockhoppers were named for the unique way they move around: while other penguins walk, this species hops about the rocky terrain.

Above and right: Chinstrap penguins wait for the right moment before safely entering the water for feeding. Often leopard seals, killer whales, and other predators swim along the shore near penguin colonies just waiting for the penguins.

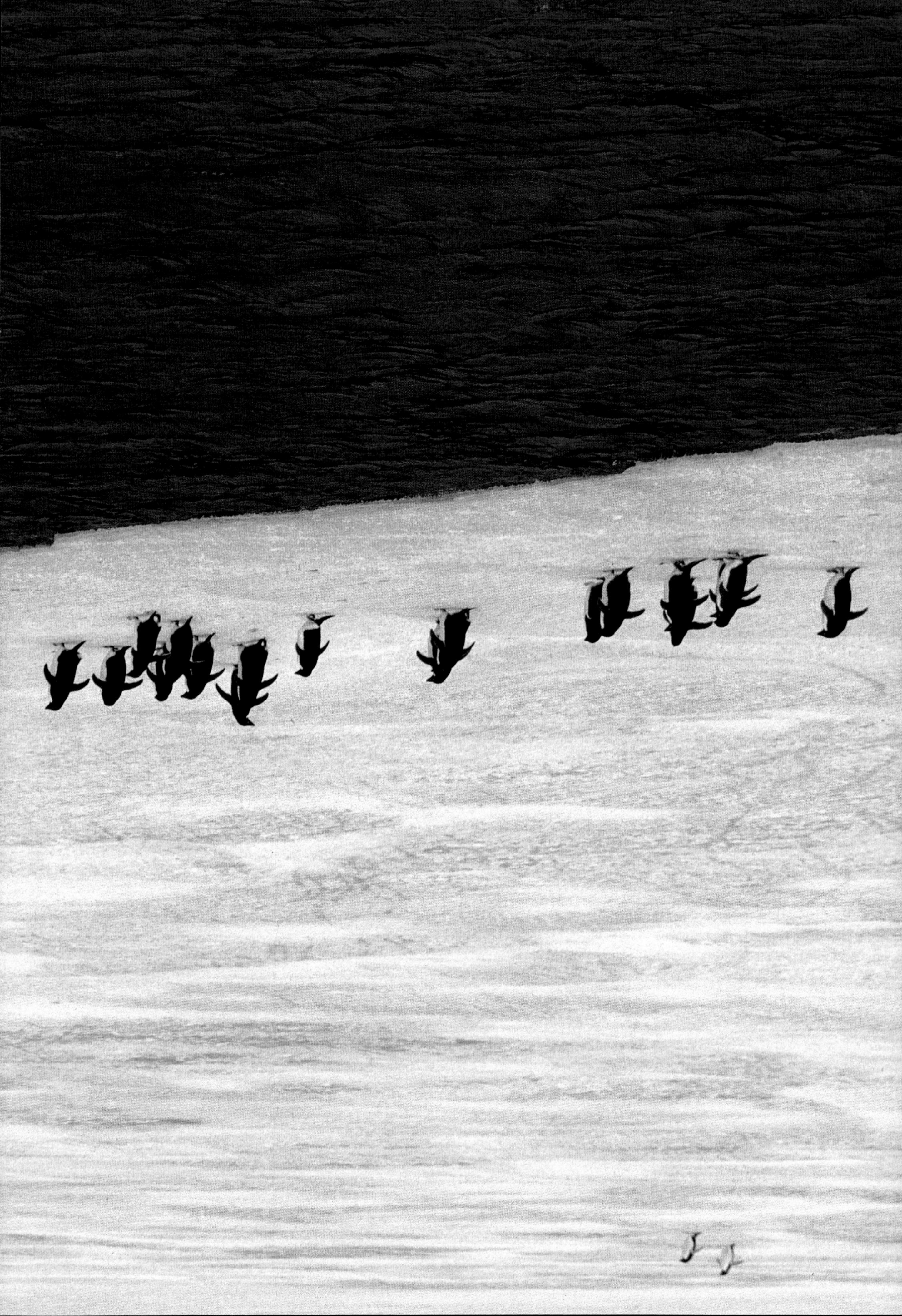

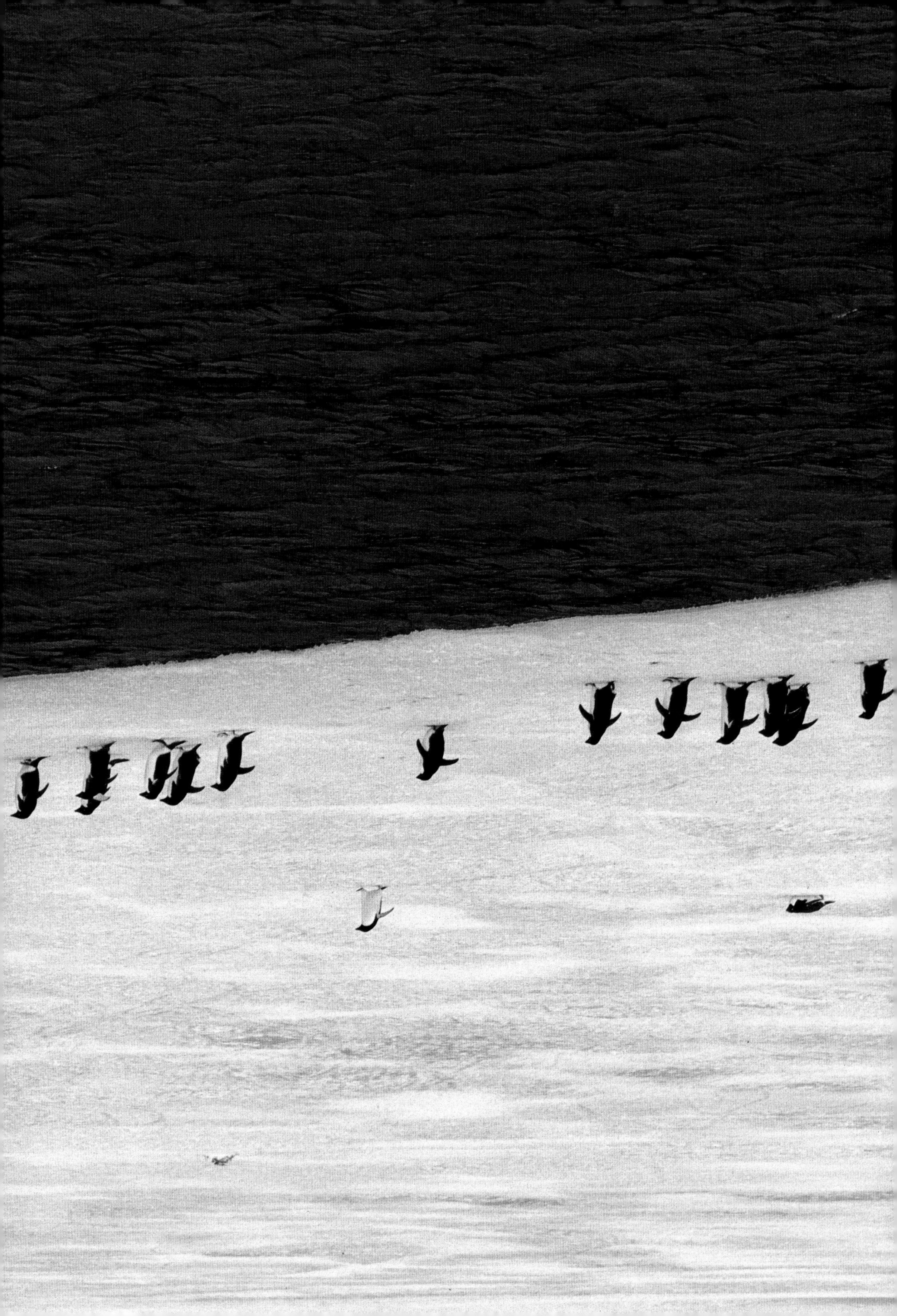

The shoreline of Paulet Island at the tip of Antarctica is covered with ice and snow, making it hard for these Adélie penguins to come ashore. Often they catapult out of the water to reach ice.

Previous pages: Adélie penguins walking along the ice edge, searching for a place to jump.

Above: Rockhopper penguins pass through tall tussock grass on the way to their colony. Rockhoppers are about twenty-one inches tall.

Magellanic penguin in tussock grass, Falkland Islands. These penguins often nest in tussock grass, burrowing into the ground for protection from predators.

Left: Chinstrap pair engaging in mutual display. Each spring, the male returns first to the same nesting site, followed by the female. They renew their relationship by a mutual display.

Above: A chinstrap engages in an ecstatic display, courtship behavior exhibited early in the breeding season to attract its mate.

Next page: A lone pair of macaroni penguins have established their nest in a rockhopper penguin colony. Species rarely mix.

41

Previous page: In Antarctica, penguins build their nests from small stones and feathers. Most penguins lay two eggs, although king and emperor penguins lay only one egg. Macaroni penguins in this small colony are still incubating their eggs at the end of November.

Above: Each species of penguin makes different sounds during the loud nest relief ceremony. Here, Adélie penguins go through a change in incubation duties. In all species, both parents take care of incubating the eggs.

Right: After one expectant parent returns from feeding at sea, the two go through a nest relief ceremony and mutual display. These chinstraps are stretching their necks toward the sky and waving their heads while they call and sing in unison.

A skua snatches a penguin egg from its inattentive parent.

A newly hatched chinstrap chick peeks out from beneath its parent. On cold days, most chicks stay burrowed beneath the warmth of a parent's cozy feathers.

At the end of December, chinstrap penguin eggs begin to hatch. The incubation period is different for each species.

These chinstrap chicks are only a few days old.

Two gentoo chicks, about one week old, beg for food from their parent.

Left: It is mid-January in Antarctica, and these chinstrap chicks are about four weeks old. One chick is reaching up to beg for food.

Above: An Adélie penguin regurgitates krill to feed its six-week-old chick. Adult penguins feed at sea, mainly on krill (small shrimp-like animals), small fish, and squid. They then return to the nest to feed their chicks.

One-and-a-half-week-old gentoo chicks trying to get as much food as they can from their parent.

Above: Penguin chicks have soft downy feathers to protect them from the cold. This Adélie chick is about four weeks old and will soon start molting.

Right and next pages: After feeding, these chinstrap chicks and parents relax at the nest. Penguins select their nesting sites on snow-free rocks or ground, so the eggs and chicks stay as dry as possible.

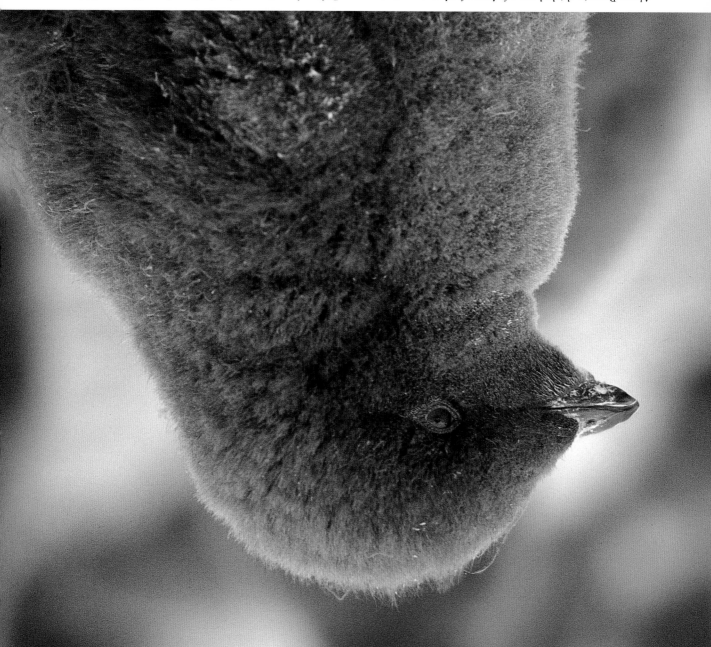

Above: Often a chick is so hungry that it runs after its parent in a wild food chase around the colony.

Right: With a belly full of krill, an Adélie chick sits near the nest. Soon the parent will return to the sea for more food.

Left: King penguin chicks develop brown downy feathers, which last around eleven months before the chicks molt and start growing juvenile feathers. This ten-month-old chick is just beginning to molt at the tips of its flippers.

Above: At the age of about eight weeks, this Adélie chick has just a little fuzzy down left. Soon it will have its complete juvenile plumage and will begin its life at sea, no longer dependent on its parents.

Left: After their chicks are raised, adult penguins go to sea to feed, then return to land to molt. During this time their feathers are not waterproof and they must remain on land. This king penguin waits on the Falkland Islands.

Above: Penguins often share beaches with elephant seals.

In a penguin colony each penguin has its own nesting territory. If a neighbor gets too close, a territorial fight may break out, as with these two chinstraps.

Left, above and next page: A southern fur seal is searching for a resting place when it approaches a nesting chinstrap penguin. Fearing for its eggs, the penguin squawks and sits tight on its nest, hoping that the seal will leave. In a fight, the penguin would not have a chance against the much larger rival.

Above: Icebergs drift at sea and slowly erode, forming spectacular shapes and awe-inspiring beauty.

Next pages: Tabular icebergs break off the Antarctic ice shelf and drift out to sea. Some are many miles long and hundreds of feet high. About four-fifths of a tabular iceberg is under water.

A group of Adélie penguins on an ice floe during their feeding at sea.

Penguins heading to the sea for feeding.

During the Antarctic summer, it stays light twenty-four hours a day. Two chinstraps are silhouetted against the Antarctic midnight sun.